LUCY

TRIES
BASKETBALL

written by

Lisa Bowes

illustrated by

James Hearne

ORCA BOOK PUBLISHERS

Lucy **loves** the park—
it's the best place to play!

Swing, climb, hide-and-seek... can we stay all day?

Ava and her cousin
are on the far court.

They're playing
basketball—
it's their favorite sport!

"Come join us, Lucy!

We'll learn from Jermaine.

He's a **professional** and **really** knows the game."

"We'll start with footwork—
you'll need busy feet.

And quick passes too—
make sure they're complete."

"Now on to **dribbling.**

Bounce the ball like so.

Right hand, then left hand.

It's a great skill to know!"

"To score in b-ball
we aim for the hoop.
Outside shots, lay-ups,

"Hold the ball up **like this.**

Now aim, then **flick your wrist.**

Keep trying, Lucy!

It's okay if you miss."

"We'll play a game next!
Teamwork is key.

Use your brand-new skills
as you play three-on-three."

"Smaller ball,
low net.
We'll use
half the floor.

And focus on fun—
no need to keep score!"

Lucy starts the play.

"I'm open!"
shouts Brett.

"Everybody back!
Now you're on defence."

Ava steals the ball.

Terrific sequence!

"A great team effort! I'm impressed," says Coach J.

"Now I'm off to work—come see the pros play!"

Lucy's keen to watch.

It's a **very** close game.

Jermaine's team **trails by two...**

The crowd chants his name!

Four seconds are left.

They're at the three-point line.

Basketball's fun to watch.
Basketball's fun to play.

Lucy, Ava and friends
hope **you'll** try it someday!

FAST FACTS!

How did basketball start?

Basketball was invented in 1891 by Canadian/American phys ed teacher Dr. James Naismith. He invented the game in Springfield, Massachusetts, as a way to keep children active during the winter months. The first basketball hoops used by Dr. Naismith were peach baskets!

What's the NBA?

NBA stands for National Basketball Association, which is one of the top professional leagues in the world. The league was founded in 1946 as the Basketball Association of America, adopting its current name in 1949 after merging with the National Basketball League.

Do you know Muggsy Bogues?

At five feet three inches tall, Tyrone Curtis "Muggsy" Bogues is the shortest player ever to play in the NBA. His autobiography is called *In the Land of Giants*.

What is three-on-three basketball?

In three-on-three basketball there are only three players on each side (in NBA basketball there are five). It is one of the world's most popular recreational sports. It was officially added to the 2020 Olympic Summer Games program.

Do you know about wheelchair basketball?

In Canada, wheelchair basketball is played by both able-bodied athletes and those with disabilities, who play alongside one another in domestic leagues. To compete for Canada internationally, though, athletes must have a disability.

Text copyright © 2019 Lisa Bowes
Illustrations copyright © 2019 James Hearne

Library and Archives Canada Cataloguing in Publication

Title: Lucy tries basketball / Lisa Bowes; illustrated by James Hearne.
Names: Bowes, Lisa, author. | Hearne, James, 1972– illustrator.

Series: Bowes, Lisa. Lucy tries sports.

Description: Series statement: Lucy tries sports

Identifiers: Canadiana (print) 20190079533 | Canadiana (ebook) 20190079509 | ISBN 9781459816978 (softcover) | ISBN 9781459816985 (PDF) | ISBN 9781459816992 (EPUB)

Classification: LCC PS8603.O9758 L824 2019 | DDC jc813/.6—dc23

Library of Congress Control Number: 2019934040
Simultaneously published in Canada and the United States in 2019

Also available as *Lucy joue au basketball*, a French-language picture book (ISBN 9781459823889)

Summary: In this picture book, Lucy and her friends learn about basketball, play three-on-three and watch a professional game.

Orca Book Publishers is committed to reducing the consumption of nonrenewable resources in the making of our books. We make every effort to use materials that support a sustainable future.

Orca Book Publishers gratefully acknowledges the support for its publishing programs provided by the following agencies: the Government of Canada, the Canada Council for the Arts and the Province of British Columbia through the BC Arts Council and the Book Publishing Tax Credit.

The author would like to acknowledge, and thank, Canada Basketball for its expertise and support.

NBA and NBA team marks are the property of the NBA and its teams. © NBA 2019. Used with permission.

Artwork created using hand drawings and digital coloring.

Cover artwork by James Hearne
Design by Teresa Bubela

ORCA BOOK PUBLISHERS
orcabook.com

Printed and bound in China.

22 21 20 19 • 4 3 2 1